friends   rain   window   flowers   birds

Monkey   umbrella   van   T-shirt   shorts   socks   bread

string   paper   red box   blue box   yellow box   sails   anchor

backpack   compass   telescope   raincoat   boots   rain hat

liner   submarine   yacht   turtles   seals

necklaces   red jewels   pearls   green jewels   sandwiches   flask

lightning   dolphins   fish   bath   soap   towel

To Adam, on your 5th Birthday

Love from,
Uncle Ian and Aunt Odette.

A Dorling Kindersley Book

Project Editor Miriam Farbey
Art Editor Jane Thomas
Managing Editor Sheila Hanly
Illustrators Judith Moffatt, Gail Armstrong
Production Louise Barratt

Photography Dave King
Additional photography Andy Crawford, Steve Gorton,
Susanna Price, Tim Ridley

First published in Great Britain in 1995 by
Dorling Kindersley Limited,
9 Henrietta Street, London, WC2E 8PS

Reprinted 1996 (twice)

A CIP catalogue record for this book is available from the British Library.

ISBN 0-7513-5304-3

Colour reproduction by Colourscan, Singapore
Printed and bound in Italy by L.E.G.O.

Acknowledgments
Dorling Kindersley would like to thank the following
manufacturers for permission to photograph copyright material:
Merrythought Ltd. for the parrot and the monkey
Margaret Steiff GmbH for the birds (p.6/7)
Ty Inc. for "Toffee" Style 2013 the dog
Carter and Parker Ltd. (Wendy Wools) for the Octopus pattern
Vera Small Designs for the sheep and lamb

Dorling Kindersley would also like to thank the
following people for their help in producing this book:
Shaila Awan, Mike Buckley, Elizabeth Fitzgibbon, Tim Lewis,
Simon Money, Hannah Moseley, Barbara Owen, and Stephen Raw.

Can you find me
in each scene?

P.B. Bear's
Treasure Hunt

Lee Davis

DORLING KINDERSLEY

LONDON • NEW YORK • STUTTGART

One morning, P.B.   woke up early. He could

hear the  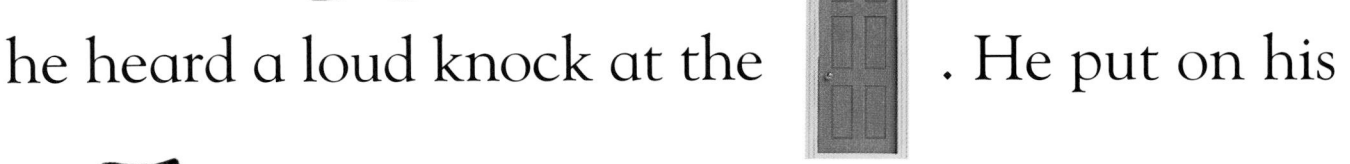 pattering against his  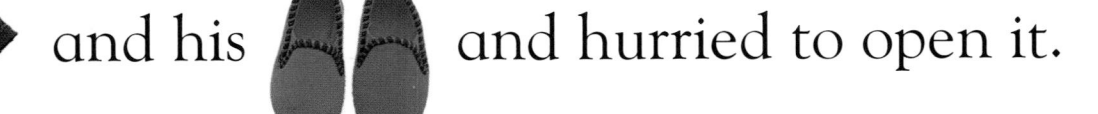. He looked

out and saw that the   were very wet.

"We're soaked through!" called some  .

"Don't come out and play until the ☀ shines."

"Oh good!" said 🧸. "I have to stay inside.

That means I can wear my 👕 a little bit longer."

But just as 🧸 snuggled back into 🛏,

he heard a loud knock at the 🚪. He put on his

🧥 and his 👟 and hurried to open it.

"A big 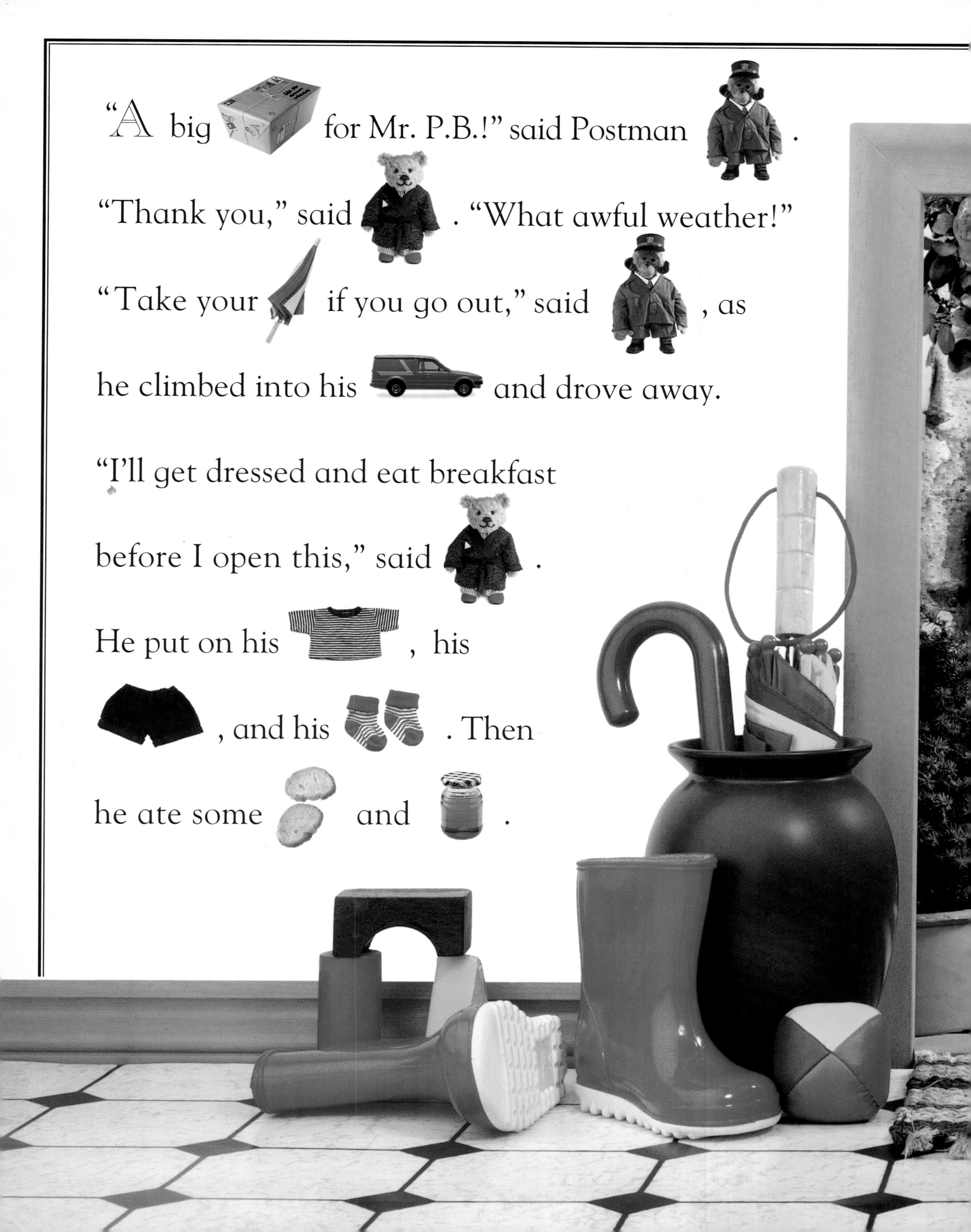 for Mr. P.B.!" said Postman .

"Thank you," said . "What awful weather!"

"Take your if you go out," said , as

he climbed into his and drove away.

"I'll get dressed and eat breakfast

before I open this," said .

He put on his , his

, and his . Then

he ate some and .

Just as  finished his breakfast there was another knock at the . He rushed to open it, and there stood his friends Dermott and Pattie .

"Hello, ," said . "We thought you'd still be in on such a rainy day. Why did you get up?"

"I've just got a great big ," answered .

"I don't know what's inside.

Can you guess?"

"Maybe it's a  from Auntie to fly to the ."

"Or a from Uncle to take us to the ."

What do *you* think is in the ?

 untied the  and tore off the  .

Inside the  was a big red  , and inside

that was a blue  , and inside that was a yellow  .

When  looked in the red  , he found

some 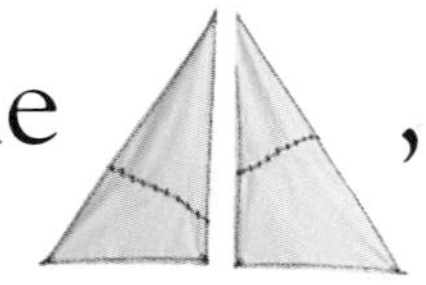  , an  , and a .

"We can build a  with these," said  ,

"but I wonder what it's for?"

"Let's look in the other boxes for clues," said  .

They found an 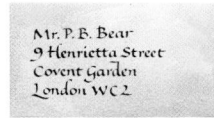 in the blue  and a  in

the yellow   . Then  opened the 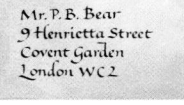 and took

out a  , a , and a 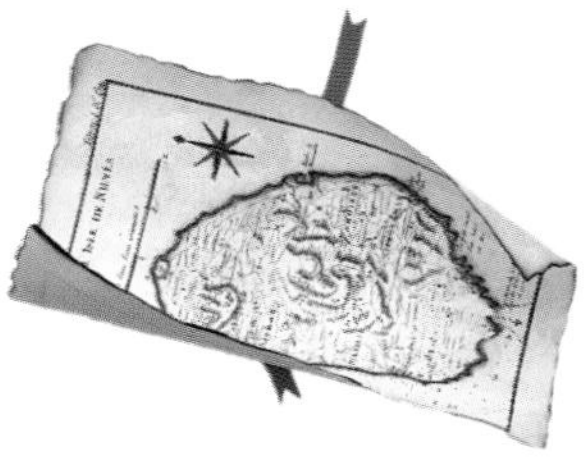 . He read the

out loud to his friends.

"Come on! Let's get

"You two build the 🚣, and I'll pack

🧭 and a 🔦 to help them find

"Is there enough food for all three of us?"

Next 🧸 put on his 👕, his

the 🖼, and the 🗝

ready to go!" shouted .

my ," said . He packed a

their way. Then he packed food for a picnic.

asked . Can you help her count?

, and his . He put the ,

in his pocket. "Let's set sail!" he cried.

The 🧸 launched the ⛵ in the river. Soon the 🐑 stopped, the ☀️ came out, and a 🌈 appeared. They sailed past a farm. "Baa baa," said the 🐑. "We've lost our baby 🐑!" Can you help the 🐑 find the 🐑?

They sailed past a [ ] . "Have a good trip," said the [ ] and the [ ] . Soon they reached the mouth of the river, where they sailed past a [ ] and out to sea.

"I'll use the  to find the island," said .

"Look! I can see a , a , and a ."

"There's a pair of friendly waving at us," cried ,

"and there are four and a huge !"

"I can spot 1 2 3 4 5 ," barked .

"One has landed on top of a ," said .

"That must be the island where the treasure is buried."

The soon reached the shore.

Help follow the clues to Oliver , who guards the treasure.

Hunt for the biggest shell on the island.

Look for four palm trees that hide what you seek.

Now cross over the bridge to Bear Island.

 showed the ▢ to ▢.

"At last!" said ▢. "Let's dig up the ▢,

then you can take me home with you."

▢ dug with his ▢ until he uncovered

the ▢. He unlocked the lid with the ▢.

Lots of ▢ and ▢ spilled out.

"Can you see four red ▢?" asked ▢.

"Look for six ▢ for me," barked ▢.

"Find eight green ▢ for me," said ▢.

"Let's take our favourite things and send the

rest to Great-Uncle Swashbuckler,"

said ▢. What would *you* take?

The  took the back to the .

"I'm hungry after all that digging," said . "Let's have

a picnic." They unpacked the , the ,

and the . After they had eaten the picnic,

collected , and played catch with a .

Then used his and

to build an enormous .

It was time for the  to go home.

As they set sail, the ☀ went behind a ☁,

the 💧💧 came pouring down, and ⚡⚡ flashed.

"Don't be scared of the storm," called some 🐬.

"Follow us!" cried some 🐟. "We'll show you the way."

At last, the reached P.B.'s house and said good-bye.

When  got inside, he took off his ▢ , his ▢ , and his ▢ . Then he took off his ▢ , his ▢ , and his ▢ . He climbed into his ▢

and scrubbed himself all over with ▢ .

He dried his fur with a ▢ and put on his favourite clothes,

his ▢ . Then he was ready to climb

into his favourite place, ▢ .

Can you count the things he brought

home from his journey?

Good night, ▢ !

P.B. Bear   Dermott   Pattie   Oliver

Sun   pyjamas   bed   door   dressing gown   slippers   parcel

honey   rocket   Astronaut   Moon   car   Clown   circus

flag   boat   envelope   key   letter   photograph   map

rainbow   sheep   lamb   castle   King   Queen   lighthouse

whale   seagulls   palm tree   treasure chest   spade   coins

apples   shells   crab   bucket   sand castle   cloud